Squishy Taylor is published by Capstone,
1710 Roe Crest Drive , North Mankato, Minnesota 56003
www.mycapstone.com

Text copyright © 2016 Ailsa Wild
Illustration copyright © 2016 Ben Wood
Series design copyright © 2016 Hardie Grant Egmont
First published in Australia by Hardie Grant Egmont 2016
Published in American English in 2018 by Picture Window Books

Library of Congress Cataloging-in-Publication Data
Cataloging-in-Publication information is
is on file with the Library of Congress.

Names: Wild, Ailsa, author. | Wood, Ben, illustrator.
Title: Squishy Taylor and a Question of Trust.
ISBN: 978-1-5158-1955-4 (hardcover)
ISBN: 978-1-5158-1971-4 (paperback)
ISBN: 978-1-5158-1967-7 (eBook PDF)

Printed in Canada.
010407F17

and a Question of Trust

Ailsa Wild

illustrated by **BEN WOOD**

PICTURE WINDOW BOOKS
a capstone imprint

For Lily Rose and Niamh — you've been helping me think about stories since you were tiny.

— Ailsa

For John. Thanks for trusting me.

— Ben

Chapter One

I'm lying on my tummy with my eye **jammed** against the telescope. I can see into an office in the building straight across from our bedroom. The office belongs to Boring Lady. She's typing away as usual. Her face looks serious.

But something is very wrong — she doesn't usually work in the middle of the night.

"What are you doing?" Vee grumbles in the bunk above me. It squeaks as she rolls over, and my eye shifts against the telescope. We have a triple bunk bed and I'm in the middle. It's awesome for doing **bunk bed tricks**, but it's the worst when you want to do night spying.

"Our bonus sister is being crazy as usual," Jessie says from beneath me.

When I first moved in here, Dad said I should think of Jessie and Vee as a bonus. I thought he was just trying to make me feel better about moving. But it turns out it's true: the twins mostly *are* a bonus. So we never say "stepsister" anymore. Bonus sisters forever.

"I'm not being crazy," I say. "I'm watching Boring Lady."

"But *Squishy*," Jessie says. Everyone calls me Squishy, even my teachers. It's a special nickname my mom and dad gave me when I was little. "Squishy, it's the middle of the night. Boring Lady isn't working."

"But that's the thing," I say. "She *is* working."

"No way!"

Vee does her Rolling-Spin-Drop move from the top bunk so she's lying beside me.

The telescope is ginormous and sits on a tripod. It's an old one from Alice, my bonus mom. Her university didn't want it anymore, so she gave it to Jessie. Jessie checks the stars and her astronomy app every night.

Vee has nudged me aside to look through the telescope. "No *way!*" she says again, but this time she's not saying it because she doesn't believe me.

"Guys!" Jessie says. "Go back to sleep. It's..." I can hear her rolling over to check the clock. "It's 2:57 in the morning."

Vee doesn't move, and her voice sounds mushed with her cheek pressed against the telescope. "Boring Lady's just typing. Like she always is. Except it's 2:57 in the morning."

"This is so weird," I say. I really love **weird stuff**. I wish there was more weird stuff in my life.

"This is so cool," Vee says.

"Go back to bed," Jessie says.

For twins, Jessie and Vee can sure act like opposites.

"I'll tell Mom," Jessie threatens.

There's no way Jessie's going to wake up Alice. Baby has been teething this week, and Alice has been getting up with him a lot at night. Alice needs her sleep.

But Vee pushes away from the telescope. She drops down into Jessie's bed, gives her a tickly squeeze, and then does the **Return-Leap-Roll**. It's a special jump we invented to get from the bottom bunk, up on the desk, across the top of the cabinet, and back onto the top bunk. It's pretty much a **ninja** move.

"Goodnight," Vee says.

I push my curls out of the way to check the telescope again, but Boring Lady has finally packed up and left. Her office light is off.

I wonder if we should stop calling her Boring Lady now that she's done something kind of interesting.

I'm nearly asleep when I hear a knocking, bumping kind of sound on the other side of the wall next to the bunk bed. **This is also weird**. Mr. Hinkenbushel, who lives in the apartment next door, is supposed to be away for work for the next month.

Chapter Two

In the morning, I wake up to the smell of smoke and the sound of screams. I do a **Drop-to-Running Descent** (always the quickest way out of my bunk) and am in the kitchen before I'm barely awake.

The **smoke** is from Dad burning pancakes, and the **screams** are from Baby. His teeth must be making him really angry this morning.

"Here," Dad says and hands the spatula

to me. Then he picks up Baby from his blanket. Baby stops crying.

I loosen the edge of the pancake and flip it. I'm an **expert pancake flipper.**

"Thanks, Squish," Dad says.

It's not until later, when we're sitting around the table having breakfast, that I remember the noises next door. I get the yucky feeling in my chest that I always get when I think about Mr. Hinkenbushel.

"Mr. Hinkenbushel came home early!" I announce.

"Oh, no," Vee says.

Mr. Hinkenbushel hates us and we kind of hate him right back. One rainy day, we were riding our scooters down the hall, and he called us **"idiot kids."** His face went all red, and he spit at us by accident from the yelling. Another time he even shouted at Alice. We were so mad at him. That's when we declared **revenge** on him.

"How do you know he's back?" Jessie asks with her mouth full.

Vee looks up from pouring about a gallon of maple syrup on her pancake.

I tell everyone about the noises in the night, but I can tell they don't really believe me.

"He said he wouldn't be back until next month," Alice says as though that settles it.

"We'll have to restart the HRC," I whisper to Vee, but Dad hears me and glares. "**Kidding!**" I say, throwing my hands in the air.

Hinkenbushel Revenge Club.

The HRC. The club was my idea. It was the first really fun thing Vee and Jessie and I did together after I moved in with them (besides hiding a runaway in our garage, which was happening at the same time). Jessie built the HRC website. We even made a revenge announcement video, which got twenty-five hits on YouTube. We started the club when Mr. Hinkenbushel shouted at Alice, so she should have been grateful. But she wasn't. Our first revenge act **totally backfired** and Alice and Dad were both pretty mad about it.

It's probably lucky they never found out about the website.

And now Mr. Hinkenbushel is back,

which is bad. It's so boring to have to be quiet every time you leave the apartment.

"All right, girls," Dad says. "This is your half hour warning."

It's Saturday. That means Alice is taking me and Vee to rock climbing while Jessie goes to violin lessons, and Dad and Baby clean the house.

Rock climbing is my new favorite thing. Mom sent me climbing clothes from Geneva, Switzerland, where she works. They're **galaxy print leggings** and a silver sports top. I like the top because it has a cross-back that makes my shoulders look strong.

I **bunch** my curls into a fat, high ponytail to keep them out of my eyes. When I'm done, I lean against the window, looking out at Boring Lady's desk. I can tell there's no one there, even without the telescope. I wonder what she was doing last night. Maybe it wasn't so strange after all. Maybe Boring Lady always types at 2:57 in the morning, but we're usually sleeping and don't see her.

Jessie is lying on her bunk with the iPad, reading the news. That's one of the weirdly grown-up things Jessie does.

"Pajamas," she says, as I'm about to leave them in a **puddle** on the floor. I had my own bedroom when I lived with my mom. I used to leave my pajamas wherever I wanted, and Mom would just laugh at me. I could have moved to Geneva when Mom got her job there with the United Nations. Instead, I moved in with Dad and Baby and our bonus family. It was the right choice — until Jessie starts telling me what to do.

I lean over Jessie to shove my pajamas under my blanket. She taps the iPad and an English-sounding man says in a slow, rich voice, *"It's absurd to suggest these diamond smugglers are operating in this city. All one has to do is look at a map!"*

Diamond smugglers? Cool. I'm almost tempted to look at whatever Jessie is listening to.

But then Alice yells from the kitchen, "Climbers! Time to leave!"

I follow her and Vee out into the hall. They're both wearing cross-back tops, too. Alice's is grey and Vee's is hot pink. Their shiny black ponytails swing in time as they walk.

On the way past Mr. Hinkenbushel's place, I see that the door is slightly open. This is weird — his door is usually

double-locked. I can't help glancing in. It's really messy inside. I wonder if he got home and just tipped his suitcase all over the floor.

I stand still for a minute, looking. **What if he's been robbed?** There's a brightly colored paper lying half out the door. It doesn't look like the kind of thing Mr. Hinkenbushel would have. I pick it up to have a closer look.

"Alice . . .?" I call, wanting to tell her about the mess. But they're straining to hold the elevator open with their hands, because the "stay open" button is broken.

I laugh and **bolt** for the elevator.

Chapter Three

"Bet I can climb the Gargoyle's Escape," Vee says as we push through the big glass doors into Rockers, the rock climbing gym. Vee always says that, but she still can't do it.

"Bet you can't," I say.

"Bet *you* can't," Vee says back.

Alice is the only one of us who's ever climbed the Gargoyle's Escape. It's the hardest section of the wall.

Rockers has a huge glass wall, so you can look out at the city if you climb high enough. I've only been climbing for a couple of weeks, but I'm almost as good as Vee already. When it's my turn, I climb fast. Sometimes when I'm climbing, I have to be really strategic and plan where to go next. But sometimes, like today, the holds seem to just appear without me thinking about it. It's like my fingers and arms are working without my brain noticing. The other cool thing about rock climbing is that it makes you better at things like the **monkey bars** and **bunk bed acrobatics**.

We take turns climbing or belaying, which is holding the safety rope, until our arm muscles ache.

Alice gives us smoothie money and sends us to catch the bus home alone while she goes on to work.

We always **race** for the shower when we get home. Vee shoves past me into the kitchen, trying to beat me. But when she sees there's a policeman sitting at the table, Vee stops. I bump into her back. Dad is frowning at the policeman.

"Whoa there, little ladies!" says the policeman like he's talking to some ponies. He chuckles as though we are **adorable** and **stupid**.

I stare at him.

"Veronica, Sita," Dad says, "this is Officer Graham." Dad only calls us Sita and Veronica when something is important. It makes me a little scared.

"What's going on?" I ask.

"Oh, nothing, nothing," Officer Graham says, resting his hands on his big stomach. "There's some kind of problem next door, so I'm talking to all the neighbors."

I think of the noises I heard in Mr. Hinkenbushel's apartment last night, and I remember the mess I saw this morning.

"Did Mr. Hinkenbushel get robbed?" I ask. I nearly add, "Serves him right." I think Dad hears my thoughts. He glares at me.

"We-ell," the policeman says. "I wouldn't say robbed, exactly. Not exactly. Ms. Jones across the hall called us because she saw the mess. We tracked down Mr. Hinkenbushel on the phone this morning. He's still away, and we located his list of valuables. None of them are missing. So it looks like vandalism."

Vee and I stare at each other. A crime on our very own floor. This is cooler than a lady typing at night.

"You two **princesses** haven't seen anything suspicious, have you?" the policeman asks. "Anyone hanging around here who might have done it? Some **bigger boys** maybe?"

Princesses? Bigger boys? Who does he think we are? I want to **choke**.

"Squishy — I mean Sita — heard a noise last night," Vee says.

I tell him about the knocking and bumping, and how I know it was after 2:57 because Jessie checked the clock.

He nods and notes it on his iPad. Jessie arrives home when I'm talking. She has her violin case slung over her shoulder. She agrees with me about when she checked the time.

"Good to know." The policeman stands up and smiles at me like my kindergarten teacher used to. "You've been very helpful, Sita." Then he chuckles. "Or should I say, Squishy?"

He's laughing at me. It doesn't feel very nice.

He shakes Dad's hand and then gives me and the girls a **stupid little wave**, like we're two-year-olds.

Dad closes the door with a solid click and turns back. His face is very serious. "OK, girls. If this has anything to do with that **ridiculous** little club of yours, tell me now."

The Hinkenbushel Revenge Club? Dad thinks WE broke into the apartment?

"Of course not," Jessie says. "That was only a game."

"We quit exactly when you told us to," Vee adds.

"It *really* wasn't us, Dad," I say.

He looks us in the eyes, one by one. "If you tell the truth now, it's much better than being caught later."

We all look right back at him. He seems satisfied.

Then Baby wakes up and starts crying, and Jessie goes to put her violin away. Vee beats me to the shower. I stand in the kitchen, thinking.

I remember the colorful paper I picked up from Mr. Hinkenbushel's doorway and dig around in my backpack to pull it out. I unfold it and spread it on the table.

It's a brochure for very beautiful, very expensive diamond rings.

Chapter Four

We're having pizza for dinner, everyone is helping. Vee is smearing tomato sauce over the crusts, Jessie is neatly adding the mushrooms, pepperoni, and olives, and I'm grating cheese for the top (and eating **pinches** of it as I go). Alice is in charge of the oven, and Dad is in charge of Baby.

The news is on. *"Police are closing in on a diamond smuggling operation, which*

sources say is operating somewhere in the center of the city. Lord Smiggenbotham has been very helpful with the police investigation."

Then a familiar, slow, rich voice comes on. *"These criminals will stop at nothing. The local police force should be very, very afraid."*

I think about our policeman and grin.

"Do you think Officer Graham is very afraid?" I ask, helping myself to more cheese. Vee slaps my hand with the sauce spoon, and tomato sauce **splatters** everywhere. We try not to giggle. Vee makes a tiny gesture, pointing to a spray of sauce on Alice's shirt, and we both try even harder not to laugh.

The reporter's voice comes back on.

"Police are seeking forged documents that declare the diamonds to be legal."

"What makes diamonds legal or illegal?" I ask.

"Well, that's a good question for your mother," Dad says. "Ask her next time you Skype."

"OK." Mom is better at answering questions anyway.

"Oh, no!" Alice says, and I think she's found the splatter on her shirt. But it's not that. "I forgot to slice the mangos," Alice says.

Vee and I groan **dramatically**. We only get dessert on Saturday nights. It's one of the **crazy rules** my bonus family has agreed on.

"Maybe we could go down to the

corner and get some ice cream?" Jessie asks. That's the thing about Jessie. She knows when to ask for things.

Alice hesitates and then sees all the pizzas, neatly lined up and ready to go into the oven. "All right," she says, and gets her wallet from her purse.

The three of us race out the door and head towards the elevator. We bang straight into Mr. Hinkenbushel.

"Hey! Watch where you're going, can't you? Rotten kids." Mr. Hinkenbushel has messy hair, and his jacket is all wrinkled. He's **scowling** at us.

"Sorry," we all say and then run for the elevator. As the elevator door closes, I see Mr. Hinkenbushel put his key into the lock and open his apartment door.

We all stare at each other. So he really is back!

We argue over whether to get chocolate or salted caramel, and Jessie wins because she's carrying the money. When we get home, we **tiptoe** past Mr. Hinkenbushel's door. We shouldn't have bothered, because he's standing in the kitchen with Alice.

"Yes, my plane arrived this afternoon," Mr. Hinkenbushel is saying. "I thought I'd better come home and get the place cleaned up."

Alice and Dad are nodding with **sympathetic faces**.

I push his diamond brochure deeper into my pocket as Jessie edges past with the ice cream to put it in the freezer.

The room smells like hot melted cheese, and I remember how hungry I am.

When Mr. Hinkenbushel leaves, **scowling**, Vee sticks out her tongue at his back. Dad gives her a warning look. I pull pieces of pepperoni off my pizza and eat them thoughtfully.

"Did Mr. Hinkenbushel say he just got back?" I ask.

Dad nods.

"Like, just this second, on the plane?" I need to get this right.

Dad nods again.

I see the image of Mr. Hinkenbushel unlocking his apartment as we got into the elevator. "But he didn't have any luggage!" I cry.

Dad and Alice don't seem to care.

But I know what my mom looks like when she gets off a plane. She always has at least two bags, one of them a big suitcase on wheels. Mr. Hinkenbushel was carrying *nothing*.

After dinner, I Skype Mom on my bed.

"Hi, my **Squishy-sweet**," she says. She's in her office because it's daytime in Geneva. She tries not to be busy at my bedtime. "What's happening?"

"The news says there are illegal diamonds in the city. Why would they be illegal?" I ask.

"Well . . ." she starts. One thing I love about my mom is that she always takes all of my questions seriously. "There are two reasons. First, diamond miners in some countries are paid very badly and work in terrible conditions. Other countries try to help the miners out by making it illegal to buy those diamonds."

I understand why Dad said to ask Mom. Her work is all about countries working together to make everybody's lives better. That's what she's trying to do at the UN.

"Second, when people bring diamonds into this country, they have to pay taxes on them. But some people smuggle them in so they don't have to pay taxes. It's greedy."

I nod. It makes me think of the brochure of expensive diamond rings I found on Mr. Hinkenbushel's doorstep. Why would Mr. Hinkenbushel even *have* a diamond brochure? Unless . . .

I hold in my excitement while I say good night to Mom. Jessie and Vee come to bed. Dad and Alice kiss us, and then they close our door. When I hear their bedroom door close, I whisper for Jessie and Vee to come sit on my bunk.

"It's Mr. Hinkenbushel," I say quietly. "He's the **diamond smuggler.**"

They both laugh at me, but I poke them. "Listen," I say. "He had no luggage just now. Why would he have no luggage? Because he was already back!"

"What?" Jessie scoffs. "He was just hanging out with the burglars?" Then she pauses thoughtfully.

I nod, even though they can't see me in the dark. "He broke into his own apartment to make it look like he wasn't there. That's why nothing was stolen!" I can feel my voice getting louder, and I have to make myself calm down so Dad and Alice don't hear us. "Plus, I found this." I hold up the diamond brochure and shine the iPad light on it. "It was in his doorway. Why would he have this?"

Jessie takes the brochure from me and turns it over. The diamonds in the photos **sparkle**, even in the dim light. She seems interested, but not convinced.

"Anyway," I say, "do you know what his job is?"

Both of them shake their heads. I don't know either. We stare at each other across the iPad light. Why would Mr. Hinkenbushel keep his job a secret? That's pretty suspicious.

Vee is getting excited. "Cool!" she says. "A real life damond smuggler!"

"You'll have to be able to prove it, though," Jessie says.

"We have to tell the police," I say.

Chapter Five

The next morning, I announce to Dad that we need to go to the police. Baby is screaming on the changing table in the bathroom, and Vee and Alice are in the kitchen arguing about homework. Vee and Alice are the only ones who ever argue about homework. Jessie does hers because she *likes* it. Dad knows that I'll do my homework on my own, and that if I have questions, I'll ask him or Alice.

"Mr. Hinkenbushel is the diamond smuggler, Dad," I say loudly over Baby's screaming and crying.

Dad wipes smears of poop off Baby's kicking legs. "What diamond smuggler?" he asks.

"The one on the news! Haven't you been listening? Lord Smiggenbotham from England is trying to find a diamond smuggler in the city, and we're sure it's Mr. Hinkenbushel. We have to tell the police right now."

Alice's voice gets louder in the other room. "Just **focus**, Veronica. You could finish this in half an hour if you tried," Alice says. **"You're not trying."**

Dad smears some cream onto Baby's bottom, which makes him scream and cry even louder.

"So, can we go to the police?" I ask.

"No," Dad says. Just like that. I don't think he even heard me properly.

"But Dad — "

"No, Sita."

"But you didn't even — "

In the other room, Vee yells, "MOM! I'M TRYING TO TELL YOU! SHE NEVER EXPLAINED IT TO ME."

"Do something useful and play with your brother," Dad says and puts Baby into my arms. **Baby stops crying** and reaches around my neck.

Dad takes my shoulders and turns me toward my bedroom. I hear him talking as he steps into the kitchen. "Cup of tea, Alice?"

Jessie is in our room on the bottom bunk. She's lying on her tummy, looking at the iPad. I plop Baby on his back next to her, and he starts pulling her hair, and giggling.

"No one will believe you," she says. "You don't have any evidence."

She nudges her nose up to Baby's and **nuzzles it** from side to side. He gurgles, and his smile gets even bigger. I love how cute Baby is.

"But the police station is around the corner," Jessie says. "We could just go."

She shows me the map. She's already done a search, and we don't even need to cross a road to get there.

Alice says we can take Baby for his walking nap in the stroller, but she makes us tell her the **Three Rules** first. We know them by heart:

1. Be quiet in the hall.
2. Don't cross any roads.
3. Never let go of the stroller.

Vee **glares** at us, and we grin back. She knows we're up to something fun, but she can't come with us. She has to finish her homework.

Baby is still gurlging happily when we get off the elevator. Soon we're on the sidewalk. I grab the stroller handle to do some **One-Foot-Slide-Scoots**.

At first,
Jessie tries
to stop me.

But Baby
is laughing, and I'm laughing,
and then Jessie is laughing too. And I'm
obeying Rule Three, so everything is OK.

As we get close to the police station door, though, I start to feel nervous.

Inside there's a big glass window with a little hole in it. I almost wish we hadn't come. A policeman steps up behind the counter. He is younger than Officer Graham and has a big smile.

"What's going on, girls?" he asks, **grinning**. "Did you find a baby?"

"No, he's ours," I say.

"Let me guess . . . you're the father?" He points at me and we all laugh.

When we stop laughing, Jessie speaks. "We're here about the diamond smuggler."

"Oh—kaaaay," the policeman says. "Hang on a minute." He types something into his computer.

"So, talk to me," he says.

Jessie nudges me. I tell him about Mr. Hinkenbushel having no luggage and how he wasn't away at all, so he must have faked the burglary himself. I show the policeman the diamond brochure I found. His lips are **pinched together**, like he's trying not to laugh, but he types in everything I say.

"Is that everything?" he asks.

I think about what the news said about the police looking for forged documents that say the diamonds are legal.

"Well, Mr. Hinkenbushel probably has the **forged documents**. They'd be in his apartment. Or a secure bank safe," I say. "Or maybe buried somewhere."

His face cracks into a huge smile, like I'm the funniest thing he's ever seen, but he's nice anyway. "Well listen, thanks for coming in." His face goes serious. "It's really important to report **suspicious** things. Even if they feel a bit . . . silly."

I can tell that he doesn't believe us.

Out on the sidewalk, Jessie pushes Baby, and I climb up and walk the fence rail by the church. I can usually take seven steps before I have to jump down, but this time I only get to three. I hate that the policeman doesn't trust us.

Chapter Six

After school on Monday, we all catch the bus home. Before I had a bonus family, Mom or Dad picked me up. Now that there are three of us, we catch the bus. Alice says we can look after each other.

The bus is empty enough to do **Upside-Down-Crazy-Legs** from the handholds, but Vee won't join me.

She's mad at us for going to the police station without her.

I do **twenty-five scissor kicks** and don't even let go when the bus stops. "Bet you can't do that," I say to Vee, stumbling down to my feet and nearly falling on her.

She does **thirty-two** and then sits with her back to me.

Jessie rolls her eyes at me and whispers, "She's been like this all day."

Jessie reminds us in the elevator to be quiet going past Mr. Hinkenbushel's door. Not that we were making any noise anyway. I slow down as we pass, but Mr. Hinkenbushel's door is closed. I feel a little bit disappointed. Maybe nothing has happened.

I'm ready for snacks and a big glass of milk, so I open our door with my key and barge into the kitchen first.

"Whoa there, girls!" says a familiar voice.

Officer Graham is sitting at the table with Dad and Alice. None of them look very happy. They've got the iPad in front of them. When I see what they're looking at, I feel sick.

It's the HRC website with our old revenge video.

They've paused the video halfway through. My face is close to the camera. My nose is wrinkled, and my eyes are all squinted up.

"Sita," Dad says. "*What were you thinking*?" He sounds very angry and disappointed. I put my head down and stare at the iPad screen.

Officer Graham taps a stumpy finger on the iPad, and the video starts playing again. It's me, saying the words that Jessie helped make up: *"We swear to bring the worst revenge on Mr. Hinkenbushel. Anything we can do to make his life worse, we will. Everything that's terrible, everything that's horrible, everything that's badder than bad, we will give him!"*

Then Vee and Jessie squash their faces next to mine.

"We swear," they both say, making **cross-eyes** at the camera.

"We will get you, Mr. Hinkenbushel!" I promise.

Then Jessie reaches forward to stop

recording. As she does, you can hear us all start to laugh.

There is **silence** in the kitchen.

Officer Graham says, "It was you three who broke into Mr. Hinkenbushel's apartment the other night, wasn't it?"

Jessie has gone white and is shaking her head.

"No!" I say. **"We would never!"**

"Well, *I* didn't," Vee says. You can already tell she's going to say something mean. "But I don't know what Jessie and Squish have been doing . . ."

Jessie and I look at Vee **in shock.** How could she say something like this?

"It really, *really* wasn't us, Dad," I say.

Dad shakes his head and points at the iPad. "This video can get you girls into a lot of trouble. You put this video and website online after you promised me and Alice that you'd give up your club. Now, **it's a question of trust.** "

"But we did give up the club. This is from before. We haven't looked at it for *months*. We'd pretty much *forgotten* about it. *Really,* Dad."

"It's true," Jessie chips in. "It says it on the YouTube page."

Dad holds up his hand. "*Enough,* Jessie. Officer Graham wants to speak with each of you, one at a time. Jessie first. Vee, go sit in your room. Squishy, our room."

They're separating us because they **don't trust us.** They think if we're together, we'll **make up lies.** For some reason that makes me feel worse than anything that's happened so far. I feel the tears choking in the back of my throat and run before everyone sees.

I lie on Alice and Dad's bed, crying into my hands. I wonder what the policeman is going to say to me. I hate that Dad **thinks we'd lie** to him about something this big. I wish Vee wasn't so mad at us. I wish my mom was here. I look around for the iPad, because I'm thinking about Skyping her. Then I realize it's busy playing the evidence for the officer in our kitchen.

I roll over and look out the balcony door to the building across the street.

Boring Lady is in her office. Typing as usual.

I get up and go out onto the balcony. I look along our outside wall. If I lean out far enough, I can almost see into our bedroom. I wish I could talk to Vee and make her understand that we didn't want to leave her out when we went to the police. I want to make sure she doesn't lie and **get us all in trouble**. If I was really desperate, I think, I could swing myself across to our window. I measure the handholds with my eyes as if I was at the rock climbing gym.

When Dad calls from the kitchen, I realize that I've accidentally locked the balcony door behind me. It doesn't matter, because I am an expert with the **bobby pin trick**. Dad says that the locks on these balcony doors are super simple. But I say it's all about skill.

I pull a bobby pin out of my hair, stick it into the lock just so, and it **clicks** right open. But this time, it isn't as fun as it usually is. My stomach has dropped down so far, it feels like it's on the floor. I don't want to talk to the police.

Chapter Seven

By the time Officer Graham finally leaves, Dad believes that we didn't break into Mr. Hinkenbushel's apartment. So does Alice. Vee didn't make up any more lies about us, but she's obviously still mad. Dad and Alice are **really mad** about the website and the video. They talk seriously about online bullying and community spirit.

They should talk to Mr. Hinkenbushel about community spirit. He's the one who shouts and won't let us play in the hall. And he's probably the one who **smuggles illegal diamonds** too.

Dad Skypes Mom, and they talk for a long time. Mom doesn't have time to talk to me before her next meeting. That doesn't feel fair. This is one time I really need to talk to her, and Dad gets all the time she has.

I lie in bed in the dark, thinking about Mr. Hinkenbushel. I wonder if the police are any closer to figuring out that he's their smuggler. Probably not. They're too worried about me and my bonus sisters being criminals.

"How are we going to catch Mr. Hinkenbushel?" I whisper.

"Go to sleep," says Jessie from her bunk underneath me.

"No one's going to believe us now," I whisper.

"**I told you!**" Jessie says. "That's because you don't have any evidence."

"That's what you get for not taking me with you to the police station," Vee says from the bunk above me. She does a **Shake-Spin-Turn-Over.** The whole bunk bed rattles.

"That has nothing to do with anything," says Jessie.

There is a pause.

"It was still **mean**, though," says Vee.

"Well, if you would have done your homework — "

"Shut UP, Jessie!" Vee half shouts. I can tell she's sitting up.

Dad's voice growls from outside our door, "I can hear you, kids."

The room seems like it echoes with all the angry words we've said.

"We just have to find the evidence," I say.

But no one answers.

In the morning, Vee isn't talking to any of us. Jessie turns on the radio news while we all eat cereal. It's boring. I try to hold

Baby on my lap and eat at the same time. I **drop yogurt** on his head, so Alice takes him from me.

Then it's the story we've all been waiting for.

"Sources say police are still seeking forged documents that they hope will lead them to the diamond smugglers. Lord Smiggenbotham suggests that the local police force might not be good enough for the job."

The familiar, slow, rich voice comes on. He sounds like he's almost laughing. *"This has to be the most bumbling, worthless police force I have ever worked with in my entire career."*

Then the reporter comes back on. *"The government says it is not considering an investigation into the local police force at this stage."*

Jessie meets my eye over the breakfast table. I think she's thinking what I'm thinking. Those forged documents might be **just the evidence we need** against Mr. Hinkenbushel. She's knows not to say anything in front of Dad and Alice. Also, there's the problem of Vee.

Vee gets on the bus at the opposite end we do. She sits there with her earphones in and her ponytail swinging back and forth. **Jessie rolls her eyes.**

I lean in to Jessie and whisper, "If

Mr. Hinkenbushel has the forged documents, where do you think he's keeping them?"

Jessie shrugs, her eyes on Vee's ponytail. Finally she says, "We need to know what he does, where he goes, understand his movements. But . . ."

I know what she's thinking again. If we get any deeper into this adventure without Vee, she's going to be so mad she might **blow up our apartment** — or the whole city.

"There's only one thing to do," I say finally. "A crazy bonus sister apology."

I stand up on the crowded bus, and shout out, **"I'm SOOO sorry, Vee!"**

She looks around. First success. I was louder than the music in her earphones.

She **scowls** and shrinks down in her seat. I push down the aisle towards her, **bonking** people with my backpack on the way through. Jessie follows, giggling and trying to hush me.

"I'm sorry, I'm sorry, I miss you!" I sing, until I'm standing in front of her, holding out my hands. The bus stops, and I almost fall over. Vee curls down in her seat, and her ears are red.

"We're sorry. Please, we need your help. And . . ." I pause for dramatic effect. **"Dog pile!"** I shout. I jump so that I'm half-sitting, half-lying on her lap. Jessie jumps on top of me. We're a heavy tangle of arms and backpacks and laughter.

"Please, please forgive us? And help us," I beg with my face in her armpit.

"Fine." Vee says. **"But get OFF me."** We scramble to our feet.

Luckily, the person who was sitting next to Vee decides to stand up, so we all squeeze together on one seat.

"OK," I whisper. I realize it's going to be very difficult to have a secret meeting now that the whole bus is watching us. I huddle in close to my bonus sisters. "How do we get evidence against Mr. Hinkenbushel?"

"We need to watch his door, and then follow him wherever he goes," Vee says.

I feel my heart relax. She's on our team again.

Jessie nods. **"A stakeout!"**

"But we can't just watch his apartment door," I object. The others agree. That would last about three minutes before Alice put a stop to it.

"The apartment entrance on the street then," Jessie says. "Let's make a list of all the reasons to hang around out front."

This is a really good plan, because Jessie likes lists, and Vee likes thinking of **ways to be sneaky**.

"Take Baby out for his nap," Vee says. Jessie gets out her notebook and writes it down. It's a good idea. But it only lasts as long as Baby is asleep.

Vee says, "Offer to run all of the errands, but then one of us stays behind to watch the front door."

Jessie writes it down, but it's the same problem. It only lasts as long as it takes to run the errands.

"Pretend we want to play outside on the sidewalk, because we're not allowed to play in the hall," Vee says.

Jessie writes it down, and smiles. Right away, we know it's pure genius. We could do that for hours.

Chapter Eight

Vee borrows sidewalk chalk from a friend at school, and Jessie Googles how to play hopscotch. By the time we get home, we're ready to start the stakeout.

I leave Jessie and Vee on the sidewalk. Then I take the elevator up with our backpacks. I tell Alice what we're doing, and she says, "Hopscotch! That was **old-fashioned** when I was in school. Have fun, and stay away from the road."

Jessie tells us what to do, because she's read the rules. She even demonstrates how to hop down the court. It's weird, because she doesn't do bunk bed moves or do rock climbing or anything sporty. I thought **hopscotch** would be a dumb game for little girls. But after we've played it for a little while, I start getting really into it. There's a **rhythm to the skip** that's satisfying.

We all keep glancing at the front door, but Mr. Hinkenbushel doesn't come or go.

I get better at not landing on the lines, and Vee is really good at tossing the stone exactly in the square. Jessie isn't as good as either of us, but she keeps playing. She doesn't seem to care that she's not as good as Vee and I are, because we have a mission. We're on a stakeout.

We do **hopscotch stakeout** after school every day, but nothing happens. We're about to give up and go to the park, when Mr. Hinkenbushel comes out the front door of our building. He walks straight past our hopscotch game and down the street.

We all stare at each other. I suddenly realize that we haven't even come up with an **excuse to follow him**.

"I'm going," I whisper.

"But — " says Jessie.

"What's the point of the stakeout if we don't follow him?"

"I'm coming too," says Vee.

"OK then, me too," says Jessie.

I shake my head. "We can't *all* go."

Mr. Hinkenbushel is getting smaller and smaller. Soon, he will disappear down the street.

"Why not?" Vee asks.

After staring at each other for a second, we all turn and run after him.

When we get closer, we slow down to a walk. I hold up my hand to mean "quiet," and we all start to tiptoe down the sidewalk. I creep along in the shadowy section of a wall, and the others follow.

Mr. Hinkenbushel looks nervous. He's going at a funny speed. Not quite fast and not quite slow, but kind of twitchy. Nervous. He's pulled a hat down over his eyes. He's **peeking out** from under it, like he doesn't want anyone to see his face. He crosses a street, and we run at full speed to make the same green light he does.

He sees something on the other side of the road. He finally slows down, so we're able to **catch up** with him. Vee pulls my sleeve and pretends to look in a shop window. We line up next to each other, our noses pressed to the window. We're trying not to laugh. It's a **really boring** display of men's shirts.

"What's he *doing*?" Vee whispers.

He seems to be dawdling. Then he suddenly picks up his pace. I realize he's following somebody too. I'm pretty sure it's a tall man with a **big gold watch** and **very shiny shoes**. The tall man has just stepped out of a bank and is walking along the sidewalk. Mr. Hinkenbushel sneaks after him, and we follow behind Mr. Hinkenbushel in a single line.

"**Who's the new guy?**" Jessie whispers from the back.

"No idea," Vee says.

"Do you think Mr. Hinkenbushel is going to do something bad?" I ask over my shoulder.

"Should we call the police?" Vee asks. She sounds nervous.

But we don't have a phone. Anyway, the police won't believe anything we say now that they've seen our revenge video.

They didn't even believe anything *before* they saw it.

Just then the tall man stops.

Mr. Hinkenbushel stops behind him, and we stop behind Mr. Hinkenbushel.

We're like **a set of dominos** ready to be tipped over.

The tall man has reached into his pocket to answer his phone.

"Good afternoon," he says, in a voice I recognize right away.

It's Lord Smiggenbotham!

Chapter Nine

At first **I'm so shocked** that I just stand there. I simply can not believe that Mr. Hinkenbushel is following Lord Smiggenbotham around!

Until this moment, part of me thought I was probably wrong. I was kind of just playing a big game with the diamond smugglers and the stakeout. But now I think it's real. Now I know **I was right.**

I pull Jessie and Vee over to a bus stop. We lean against the glass, pretending to wait for the bus. Mr. Hinkenbushel is nearby, pretending to be in line at a coffee stand.

But really, **we're all listening** as hard as we can to what Lord Smiggenbotham is saying during his phone call.

"This is absolutely our last chance," he says into his phone. His rich voice sounds less lazy than usual. "If we don't make our move tonight . . ." Then he pauses. "If you cannot manage to locate the documents, then I shall do it alone." He **hangs up and scowls** down at his phone. "Utterly useless," he mutters.

"It sounds like he's very angry with the police," I whisper.

Jessie nods. "Well, they're not doing a very good job."

I wonder what Mr. Hinkenbushel will do now. He's turned around. His hat is off now, and **he's almost strutting**. He actually looks quite pleased with himself. It almost looks like he *wants* to be seen. We trail behind him, but he goes straight home. Jessie and Vee and I look at each other, confused. Why did he even go out in the first place?

Mr. Hinkenbushel stops in front of our building to answer his phone.

Jessie silently passes me the hopscotch stone. I toss it and start hopping. I don't even have to **strain my ears** to hear what Mr. Hinkenbushel is saying now.

"I'm out. I'm catching a plane out of

town this evening," he says loudly. "For a meeting, but I'll be back tomorrow." He pauses. "Yes, the document is in my apartment, all safe."

Then he nods, hangs up, and glances down the street. I follow his gaze. Was that Lord Smiggenbotham I saw ducking round the corner?

Mr. Hinkenbushel looks pleased for some reason, and he goes inside. Is he pleased because of the phone call? Or did he do something we didn't notice to Lord Smiggenbotham?

We wait until the elevator doors close. "The document!" I say. "It's right there, *next door to us.*"

Jessie shakes her head. "He could have been talking about any document."

"We just caught him following Lord Smiggenbotham!" I say. "Of course it's the document."

"Are we 100% sure that was Lord Smiggenbotham he was talking to?" Jessie asks.

"A million % sure," I say.

We all nod. We've heard his voice enough times on the news.

"But they didn't talk to each other," she says. "It *could* have been a coincidence that they were in the same place at the same time."

"But it wasn't," Vee says.

We all nod again. Mr. Hinkenbushel went looking for Lord Smiggenbotham on purpose. Then he made sure that Lord Smiggenbotham saw him. Then he walked away from Lord Smiggenbotham. We just don't know why.

Dinner isn't quite ready, so I lie on the family room floor with Baby. I give him my finger to grip and pull his little fist around. But I'm not really paying attention to Baby. I'm thinking.

Mr. Hinkenbushel is going out of town tonight, and his apartment will be empty. The police and Lord Smiggenbotham don't know where to find the document that will lead them to the diamond smugglers. The document is in Mr. Hinkenbushel's apartment, **which will be empty** . . .

I Skype Mom.

She coos at Baby and tries to make him clap, but he just wiggles his hands at her. He's not coordinated enough to clap yet. Then **he tries to eat the iPad**, so I leave him on the blanket. I take the iPad into our room.

"Mom, those diamond mines. Are they really bad?" I ask.

"Yeah, Squishy." She nods. "They're really bad."

"OK." She's helping me make a decision, even though she doesn't know it. "And, Mom, what would you do if the police didn't believe you, but you knew you were right?"

Mom **suddenly looks suspicious.** "Is this about that revenge club thing? Have the police been there again? Do I need to speak with your father?"

I forgot that she just found out today about the HRC video. Of course she's still worried.

"Mom, it's *fine*, nothing else has happened."

"Are you sure?"

"I'm sure," I say.

"This is about something different." I make up a little lie. "It's a thing I'm doing for school . . . about . . . um . . ." I stop to think. "It's about justice."

She still looks suspicious, but also thoughtful. "What was your question? What would I do if the police didn't believe me?" She thinks it over. "Is it about something important?" she asks.

I nod.

"I suppose . . ." She's still thinking. "I suppose I'd do everything I could to **prove I was right.**"

Chapter Ten

It's really late. Dad and Alice have gone to bed, and Baby has stopped crying.

It's time.

"Vee," I whisper. "Let's do it."

"Whaaa . . .?" Vee sounds groggy. She must have been asleep.

I hear Jessie sit up. "You two are **bam–bam crazy**," she says.

I'm already pulling my pajamas off. I've got my climbing clothes underneath.

We planned it all after dinner. I get to be the one, even though Vee's been climbing longer than me. I thought she'd argue more. But after she looked down out the window, she went a little white and let me.

While I tie myself into the climbing harness we made, Jessie says all the things she said before we went to bed.

"You'll fall. **You'll die**. There's nothing there anyway. The police will come and put you in jail."

Vee anchors the rope around the bedpost and holds it, ready to belay me. My harness is made of climbing rope and a leather belt, and it's **really strong**.

"I won't fall," I say. "Vee's got me. Don't you, Vee?"

Vee nods, biting her lip.

"It's a question of trust," I say. I'm grinning and afraid at the same time.

I open the window. Jessie goes quiet and stands behind Vee to hold the rope.

I climb out onto the windowsill. The ground is a really long way down. Even the tops of the trees are a really long way down. **My heart starts thundering,** my throat blocks up, and I feel like my forehead is burning from the fear.

I know my harness is good, and I can feel the strength of Vee's hands on the end of the rope. It's only six feet across to the balcony. The handholds are easier than the easiest wall at the climbing gym. This is nothing.

Suddenly, it doesn't **feel** like nothing.

It feels like **the scariest thing** I have ever, ever done.

But I can't climb back inside now.

I reach along the wall for the first brick and curl my fingers around it. It feels solid. I can do this. I have to trust myself. I nudge my toe out and find a hold.

My fingers feel strong, and I know what I'm doing. I **inch spider-ways** across the wall. I'm trying not to think about the drop. I'm trying not to think about being an idiot and Jessie being right. I'm just feeling the gentle tug of the rope that tells me Vee is holding on. I try to focus on the strength in my fingertips.

I reach the balcony rail and swing myself over it onto the tiles. I collapse and just sit there feeling sick. I already

know that was not just the scariest but also the stupidest thing I've ever done. You'd think I'd be relieved that I didn't die. But I'm not. Also, I know I have to do the whole thing again to get back.

"You OK?" Jessie hisses from the window.

"Yep," I say. **"Shhh."**

If Alice and Dad wake up and realize what we're doing, they'll probably disown us. They'll send us to a boarding school for naughty children who misbehave. Or maybe they'll just feed us to a bunch of **hungry sharks**. And Mom would fly back from Geneva to help them.

I make myself stand up and unclip the harness. Mr. Hinkenbushel's balcony door is exactly the same as Alice and

Dad's, but it opens into a living room instead of a bedroom. I'm glad, because I do *not* want to see Mr. Hinkenbushel's underwear lying on the floor.

I point my flashlight around his living room. There's not much here. The next room is an office with bookshelves full of folders and a computer on a desk with papers everywhere. I know this is **where I need to look** for the document. I think whatever I'm looking for must be very well hidden, so I'm ready to do a thorough search.

But the first thing I see, as though it's been placed there for me to find, is an official-looking paper. **It's a receipt.**

"*The Shiny Mine Diamonds, purchased in the amount of . . .*" I stare at the number printed on the page. The row of zeros blur, and I can't even count them all.

I found it. The document the police are looking for. It was way too easy . . .

Then I hear a noise that makes my heart feel like it's going to **jump out of my mouth.**

Someone is turning the handle of Mr. Hinkenbushel's front door!

Chapter Eleven

I stand there gripping the receipt as a **key turns** and the **lock clicks** open. Mr. Hinkenbushel is home early. I look around fast. I don't have time to run to the balcony and climb back across. Maybe I could hide under the desk? Or what if I just stand really still? I turn off the flashlight and press against the wall. Maybe he won't come into the office.

But he does. **It's strange.** He

doesn't turn on the light. He just walks straight to the office doorway and stands there. He has a **tall and scary** shadow. In fact, he's really tall. He's much taller than Mr. Hinkenbushel. His silhouette looks familiar, but it's definitely not our grouchy neighbor.

He turns on his flashlight and starts to rummage through the papers on the desk. I suddenly realize who it is.

"Lord Smiggenbotham!" I say with a feeling of relief.

He gives **a little scream** and drops his flashlight.

"It's just Squishy Taylor," I say, turning on my own flashlight, and shining it at him. "I live next door. I've been trying to catch him too."

Lord Smiggenbotham squints in the flashlight beam and shades his eyes. "Trying to catch . . . who?" he asks.

"Mr. Hinkenbushel, the diamond smuggler!" I say. "And I think I've found what you're looking for. It's the forged receipt, right?" I wave the paper out in front of me.

Lord Smiggenbotham picks up his flashlight and stares at me strangely. Then he shakes his head. "Good gracious, yes. Mr. Hinkenbushel, the diamond smuggler!" He smiles an odd kind of smile and snatches the receipt out of my hands. "Have you read this?" he asks, looking at me sharply.

"Enough to know it's a receipt for *very* expensive diamonds," I say.

"But not . . ." He checks himself and looks it over. "Ah, yes. This is just the thing. The police will be delighted. I shall just . . . go now . . . to the police station. I'll be sure to let them know what a very **good little girl** you are."

He's backing out of the room.

I hate being called a "good little girl". But this might work to my advantage.

"Hey, Mr. um, Lord? What do you think about coming next door and telling my parents that I was right and everything's OK. Otherwise I have to do that **horrible climb** back across to my bedroom. Come on."

I grab his hand and start to pull him out the door and down the hall toward our apartment.

"Well, I'd much rather . . . um . . . my goodness," he says.

And suddenly, we are both staring Alice in the face.

"What is going on?" Alice asks. Our door is wide open, and all the lights are on inside. Baby is in her arms, blinking and spitting.

Behind her, Vee mouths, "Busted."

"Ah . . . um . . . This very good little girl has been helping me with my police investigations into the diamond smuggling situation."

Alice looks down at the tangled rope of my homemade climbing harness, and her eyes widen. She opens her mouth to ask a question.

"So sorry to disturb you in the middle

of the night. I think I'll just leave now . . ." Lord Smiggenbotham starts to say, and trails off.

"I'm going to need a much better explanation than that," Alice says to him in her stern **"Mom-voice."**

The elevator dings, and the doors open. It's Mr. Hinkenbushel. **"Perfect!"** I say to Lord Smiggenbotham. "Now you can arrest him, and then we can all go back to bed."

Lord Smiggenbotham backs away from us. "What? Huh?" Then he pulls himself up and turns to Mr. Hinkenbushel. "You, sir, are a diamond smuggling criminal," he declares.

To my surprise, Mr. Hinkenbushel grins. "No," he says. **"You are."**

Behind us, the stairwell door opens. A woman comes striding towards us.

"Lord Smiggenbotham. I'm placing you under arrest for theft, fraud, and breaking and entering."

Vee, Jessie, and I stare at each other in complete disbelief.

It's Boring Lady.

She turns Lord Smiggenbotham around and handcuffs him.

"That was a job well done," she says to Mr. Hinkenbushel, who grins again. It's practically a high five.

Chapter Twelve

"But I . . . I thought *you* were the diamond smuggler," I say to Mr. Hinkenbushel.

"And I thought *you* were just annoying children." He looks around at all of us. "No — it turns out you're not just annoying. You're nosy, dangerous, and you almost got yourself killed ruining the **secret undercover operations** trap I set for Lord Smiggenbotham."

My stomach sinks.

"Goodness gracious," says Lord Smiggenbotham. He sounds desperate and not quite so rich now, with his nose pressed up against the wall. "I'm not the criminal you're after, my good man! I'm on your side."

"Nonsense," Mr. Hinkenbushel growls. "You've been using your special access to the police to hide your crimes. But you just aren't clever enough to get away with it forever."

"My, the police around here are rather rude, aren't they?" Lord Smiggenbotham sneers. I can tell he knows he's been defeated for good.

Boring Lady gives him a shake. "That's enough, Lord Smiggenbotham. Let's get you down to the police station."

Boring Lady pulls a card from her pocket and hands it to Alice. "I'll let you get back to sleep. But come by in the morning, and bring the girls," she says. **"We'll want to question them."**

Mr. Hinkenbushel follows Boring Lady, who pushes Lord Smiggenbotham down the hall to the elevator.

I can **hear him complaining** as they walk away. "Careful of my shirt, it wrinkles easily."

We are all left standing in the hall — Alice, Baby, my bonus sisters, and me. I'm trying to take off my harness so Alice doesn't notice it.

Alice reads what's on the card Boring Lady gave her. "Chief of Special Secret Undercover Operations," she says. Chief? Secret? Undercover? Boring Lady **isn't so boring after all!**

Dad stumbles out, squinting at the light, and asks, "What's going on?"

The rest of us look at each other and then burst out laughing. **Even Baby.**

The next morning, Alice takes us to meet the Chief of Special Secret Undercover Operations. **Not-Boring Lady** (that's what we call her now) takes us to a big room with a shiny wooden table.

She shakes all our hands. "Thank you for coming," she says.

We haven't stopped talking since we woke up. Mr. Hinkenbushel is an **undercover agent!** The receipt was in his apartment the whole time!

I have so many questions, I start talking before we even sit down. "But how did you and Mr. Hinkenbushel already have the receipt?" I ask.

"Squishy!" Alice says.

But Not-Boring Lady nods. "Good point. Mr. Hinkenbushel took it a few weeks ago, while he was undercover, pretending to be a criminal from a different gang. So the smugglers thought **they had been tricked** by other criminals, not caught by the police."

"*That's* why you told the news you were still looking for it!" Jessie says. "To protect Mr. Hinkenbushel's disguise." She pauses. "But who broke into his apartment the first time?"

Not-Boring Lady smiles. "You are quick, aren't you? It was the smugglers, trying to get their receipt back. Luckily, I was keeping it safe."

"**I don't get it,**" I say. "You had

the receipt. Wasn't that all the evidence you needed?"

"But it didn't prove that Lord Smiggenbotham was bringing illegal diamonds into the country. So we used the receipt as bait," she says. **"To catch him red-handed."**

Jessie realizes something. "So Lord Smiggenbotham was *meant* to hear Mr. Hinkenbushel say he was going out of town, leaving the receipt in his apartment."

Not-Boring Lady grins. "But you heard him too. Tell me, how *did* you end up in the middle of a special police operation?"

She asks us lots of questions and we all **talk over ourselves** trying to answer them. We tell her about the diamond brochure and the hopscotch stakeout and the homemade harness.

When she finally seems satisfied, I ask, "Will he have to pay his diamond taxes now?"

"Yes. Plus a big fine. He might even go to prison," Not-Boring Lady says.

Vee can't wait anymore to ask, **"But where are the diamonds?"**

"Ah!" Not-Boring Lady says. "We got the diamonds first. They're what made us realize there *were* smugglers operating in the city. Follow me."

She leads us down a long hall into an elevator, down to a basement, through a big cage door with a key card lock, and into a room with lots and lots of safes. It's like something out of a **movie.**

Every safe has a big dial.

She turns one dial this way and that way. Then she opens the door. She takes out a silver suitcase and puts it on a table.

Inside is a plastic bag full of tiny clear stones. They are a little bit shiny. But they don't look *that* special.

"I thought they would be **big** and **sparkly**. These are so little." I say.

I think about how stupid it is that stones so small and ordinary could make someone want to steal and lie and be cruel to people.

"What happens to the diamonds now?" Vee asks.

"Mr. Hinkenbushel will return them to the miners. They can sell them to buy food for their families."

I'm thinking Mr. Hinkenbushel might be a nice man after all. But just then, the cage door beeps and Mr. Hinkenbushel comes in. He **scowls at us** and at the suitcase of diamonds.

He obviously thinks showing them to us is a terrible idea.

"Good morning, ma'am," he says to Not-Boring Lady. "I'm signing these out."

He puts the diamonds away and closes the suitcase. Then he takes it over to a desk on the other side of the room and starts filling out a form.

Not-Boring Lady grins at us. "He's a **cranky-pants**," she whispers. "But he's good at his job."

As we're stepping out onto the street, I turn back to Not-Boring Lady. "If you're the chief, how come you just type at your computer all the time? Why don't you act like a spy?"

"Squishy!" Alice says, embarrassed.

Not-Boring Lady waves a "don't worry about it" hand to Alice, and turns to me. "I have all my meetings in the big room. Your window looks into my quiet office. No one's allowed to disturb me there *ever*." She laughs. "I guess I would be pretty boring to watch."

That night, Dad talks to Mom for a long time before I'm allowed to. When he **finally** comes out of his room and hands me the iPad, Mom's smiling. But she also looks a little serious.

"It sounds like you'll have to take me rock climbing when I come home," she says.

I can tell she's worried by the stuff Dad told her.

"Squishy, I'm glad I taught you to be brave and take risks, but . . ." She pauses.

"But be careful?" I suggest.

She grins. **"Please be careful."**

"Don't worry, Mom. I will."

I get into bed first. Jessie tucks herself in the bunk beneath me, and Vee does a big, fast, **Clambereeno** up to her bunk.

I lie on my tummy, staring out at Not-Boring Lady's office. The light is off, but now I know she might just be in the big meeting room.

I think about the basement room with the safe and the diamonds. I think about special operations and criminals being caught red-handed. **By me**. I grin into the dark. Weird stuff. I love weird stuff.

About the author and illustrator

Ailsa Wild is an acrobat, whip cracker, and teaching artist who ran away from the circus to become a writer. She taught Squishy all her best bunk bed tricks.

Ben Wood started drawing when he was Baby's age, and happily drew all over his mom and dad's walls! Since then, he has never stopped drawing. He has an identical twin, and they used to play all kinds of pranks on their younger brother.

Glossary

bonus (BOH-nuhs)—an extra reward or benefit

evidence (EV-i-duhns)—information and facts that help prove something is true or not true

forge (forj)—to make a copy of something, such as money or a person's signature

fraud (frawd)—dishonest behavior and tricks that are intended to deceive people or get money from them

operation (ah-puh-RAY-shun)—a well-organized plan that involves a lot of people

smuggle (SMUHG-uhl)—to bring things into or out of a country illegally

stakeout (STEYK-out)—when police watch a location waiting for a crime to happen or for or a criminal to arrive

suspicious (sus-SPISH-ush)—thinking that something is wrong or bad, but having little or no proof to back up your feelings; giving the impression of being wrong, untrustworthy, or dangerous

tax (taks)—money that people and businesses must pay in order to support a government

United Nations or UN (yoo-NAY-tid NAY-shuns)—an organization that includes almost every country in the world that was formed in 1945 to promote international peace, cooperation and security

vandalism (VAN-duhl-iz-uhm)—the deliberate damaging or destruction of someone's property

Talk About It!

In this story, Squishy and her bonus sisters have broken their parent's trust. In what ways have they done this? How did they earn their parents' trust back?

The police find the website and video the girls made for their revenge club. Do you think this is online bullying? Have you ever experienced online bullying?

Are Mr. Hinkenbushel and the Boring Lady (Chief of Special Secret Undercover Operations) happy for Squishy's and the bonus sisters' help in the investigation? Did they need the girls' help? Why or why not?

Write About It!

Squishy climbs over to Mr. Hinkenbushel's apartment and puts herself in great danger. Write about one thing that could have gone wrong during Squishy's climb.

Why does Squishy suspect Mr. Hinkenbushel is the smuggler? List all the clues that Squishy finds.

How do the girls feel when the grown-ups don't believe them? What proof do they find to convince the grown-ups they are right? Write about a time when you had to prove you were right to a grown-up.

It's **Squishy Taylor**

She's a GENIUS mystery-solver and sneakier than a ninja!

You're going to **love her!**

An apartment full of questions on a street full of mysteries...

Why is her next-door neighbor the **CRANKIEST** man in the world?

What do you do when everyone **HATES** your hero?

What kind of person comes back from a trip with **NO** luggage?

How do you get rid of a Chinese-warrior **GHOST?**

HAVE **YOU** READ EVERY **SQUISHY TAYLOR** BOOK?